Read-Along
STORYBOOK AND CD

The Easter-Egg Hunt

This is the story of Winnie the Pooh and the Easter-egg hunt. You can read along with me in your book. You will know it is time to turn the page when you hear a chime, like this. . . .

Let's begin now.

Printed in the United States of America

First edition 10 9 8 7 6 5 4 3 2 1

V381-8386-5-09258

Library of Congress Control Number: 2009906399

ISBN 978-1-4231-2087-2

Visit www.disneybooks.com

New York

Certified Chain of Custody
35% Certified Forests,
65% Certified Fiber Sourcing
www.sfiprogram.org

It was a beautiful spring day in the Hundred-Acre Wood. As Winnie the Pooh walked toward Rabbit's house for an Easter-egg hunt, he heard a rumbling in his tumbly. He had eaten just a few minutes earlier, but it felt as if it were a long time ago.

Then Pooh had a worrisome thought—what if Rabbit was out of honey? He stopped to ponder.

Finally, he decided to hurry back home and get a jar. He didn't want to show up to the Easter-egg hunt empty-handed.

When Pooh finally arrived at Rabbit's house, he was, in fact, empty-handed—except for a straw basket.

Pooh had realized he couldn't hunt for Easter eggs while carrying a jar full of honey. So he had stopped and eaten every last drop. After all, he didn't want it to go to waste.

Pooh spotted his friends. He wondered why it seemed as if they had been waiting for a while. He had left exactly on time. "Happy Easter!"

Pooh's friends were excited to see him. "Happy Easter!"

Rabbit hopped onto a tree stump. "Everyone, I have hidden Easter eggs all over the woods. Whoever finds the most will win a special feast. Get ready, get set . . . go!"

"Today is going to be an *egg*-cellent day!" Tigger seemed very excited. "Tiggers love contests."

Pooh, Piglet, Roo, Kanga, and Eeyore walked into the woods.
Tigger bounced off in another direction. "Good luck, everyone!"
    Pooh knew that Rabbit was a good Easter-egg hider. Pooh wanted
to be an even better Easter-egg *finder*.

Pooh rubbed his chin and scratched his tummy. "Hmm . . . if I were Rabbit, I would hide an Easter egg in . . ." Pooh trailed off when he saw some yellow flowers. "Daffodils!" He felt the ground under the leaves.

"A yellow egg!" Pooh put it into his straw basket.

"I shall show this to all my friends!" Pooh hurried off. Piglet would be so surprised!

But Pooh did not know his Easter basket had a hole in the bottom. The yellow egg had fallen out onto the grass.

Piglet was not far behind Pooh. Soon he found the yellow egg. "Oh, my, lucky me!" He did not know that Pooh had found it first. Piglet carefully tucked the egg into his own Easter basket.

Pooh looked behind a tree and underneath a blackberry bush. Then he found something behind a rock. "A purple egg!"

Pooh placed it in the basket and began to daydream about all the delicious honey he would eat if he won. At least he hoped it would be honey. After all, Rabbit had only said "feast."

He didn't notice when the egg slipped out of the basket.

Not far behind, Roo hopped by the blackberry bush and the rock. He hadn't found a single egg yet. Roo began to hop slower and slower. Finally, he stopped and heaved a big sigh. He looked down at the grass. There was Pooh's egg! "Oh, goody! Purple is my favorite color!"

Meanwhile, Pooh found a green egg in a tall clump of grass. "This may very well be the luckiest Easter ever!"

The egg fell out of the basket.

A little while later, Tigger was bouncing along when he saw a large, green egg. But he had no idea it had fallen out of Pooh's Easter basket. Tigger stopped bouncing long enough to pick it up. "*Hoo-hoo-hoo-hoo!* I'm on my way to winning!"

Pooh carefully looked through a bed of pink wildflowers. It was
the most curious thing. The flowers smelled just like a fresh jar
of honey. Then he spotted a red egg on the ground.

"That honey smell reminds me. I think it is nearly time for a
snack." Pooh rubbed his rumbly tummy thoughtfully.

Before long, Eeyore rambled by the pink flowers. He had not especially wanted to look for Easter eggs. It was all such a lot of work. Then he spotted Pooh's red egg and supposed it would be rather nice to win Rabbit's contest.

Nearby in a meadow, Pooh began to think of the delicious feast that Rabbit had prepared. It was almost time to return.

He tucked one last egg into his Easter basket.

As Pooh walked up a hill toward Rabbit's house, the egg fell out and rolled away!

Kanga was on her way back to Rabbit's house, too. She had not found any eggs, but she did not mind. She thought the hunt had been great fun, and she had worn her Easter hat for the occasion. Just then, she saw the blue egg next to a log and picked it up.

Soon everyone was back at Rabbit's house. Rabbit stood up on top of a tree stump. "Time is up!"

Piglet showed his friends the yellow egg he had found. Roo took out a purple egg.

Tigger held a large green one. "I pounced, bounced, and triple-trounced until I wrestled this egg to the ground!"

Eeyore displayed his red egg. Then Kanga showed her pretty blue egg.

Finally, it was Pooh's turn. He looked inside his straw basket—it was empty! Pooh wondered where all his Easter eggs had gone. He turned the basket upside down and shook it. But nothing came out. "Oh, bother! Perhaps the eggs decided to hide again."

Piglet looked at the basket in Pooh's hands and poked his hand through the opening. It looked just the right size for an egg to fall through. "Oh look, Pooh Bear. There's a hole in this basket."

"Pooh, you may have my yellow egg. It might have been yours before it was mine." Piglet held the egg out.

Pooh smiled at his friend. "Why, thank you, Piglet."

Roo hopped forward. "You can have mine, too."

Pooh didn't want his Easter eggs to hide again, so he set the basket on the ground and held the eggs.

"Here, buddy bear. Tiggers like to win fair and square." Tigger added his green egg to the ones in Pooh's arms.

Eeyore thought finding such a pretty egg was probably too good to be true, so he gave his to Pooh. Then Kanga brought her bright blue egg to Pooh and gently placed it on the very top of the pile.

"Pooh has the most eggs!" Roo hopped up and down eagerly. "He must have won!"

Rabbit walked over to Pooh. Suddenly, the red egg began to wobble. Rabbit caught it as it fell and put it on the ground. Then he counted up all the eggs. "One . . . two . . . three . . . four . . . five. Pooh is the winner!"

Then Pooh realized something. His friends had shared their eggs with him. If he had won an Easter feast, he wanted to share it with them. He was feeling very hungry, though. "Is there enough for everyone?"

Rabbit grinned. "Of course. I thought we should all celebrate Easter together."

Pooh was still worried. Rabbit had not said anything about Pooh's favorite food. A feast wasn't a feast without it. "Is there enough honey?"

"I always keep lots of honey on hand. You never know when a Pooh Bear will show up." Rabbit dashed into his house.

"Hurray!" Pooh put down his Easter eggs very carefully.

Pooh and his friends had a great feast.

Tigger made an announcement. "This was the most *egg*-cellent Easter ever, *egg*-specially the egg hunt!"

Pooh would have agreed, but he was too sticky to do anything except nod. It had been a wonderful Easter, indeed.